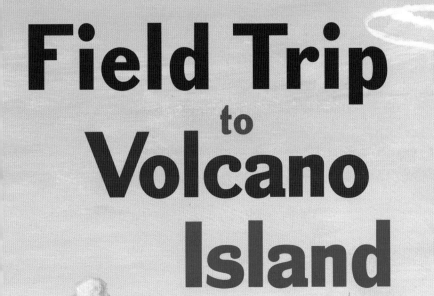

Field Trip
to
Volcano
Island

by JOHN HARE

MARGARET FERGUSON BOOKS
HOLIDAY HOUSE · NEW YORK

To Sherry—because flowers don't last
and words aren't enough.

Margaret Ferguson Books
Copyright © 2022 by John Hare
All Rights Reserved
HOLIDAY HOUSE is registered in the U.S. Patent and Trademark Office.
Printed and bound in October 2021 at Toppan Leefung, DongGuan, China.
The artwork was created with acrylic paint.
www.holidayhouse.com
First Edition
10 9 8 7 6 5 4 3 2 1

Library of Congress Cataloging-in-Publication Data

Names: Hare, John, (Children's book illustrator), author, illustrator.
Title: Field trip to volcano island / John Hare.
Description: First edition. | New York : Holiday House, 2022. | "Margaret
Ferguson Books." | Audience: Ages 4 to 8. | Audience: Grades K–1.
Summary: "In this wordless picture book, a student is accidentally left
behind on a field trip to a volcano island"— Provided by publisher.
Identifiers: LCCN 2020054249 | ISBN 9780823450428 (hardcover)
Subjects: CYAC: School field trips—Fiction. | Volcanoes—Fiction.
Islands—Fiction. | Stories without words.
Classification: LCC PZ7.1.H3675 Fim 2022 | DDC [E]—dc23
LC record available at https://lccn.loc.gov/2020054249

ISBN: 978-0-8234-5042-8 (hardcover)